P9-CJF-495

RAYMOND BRIGGS
The Snowman

RANDOM HOUSE 🏠 NEW YORK

Copyright © 1998 by Raymond Briggs.
Illustrations by Maggie Downer, based on the the book THE SNOWMAN by Raymond Briggs.
All rights reserved under International and Pan-American Copyright Conventions.
Published in the United States by Random House, Inc., New York.
ISBN 0-679-89215-X

www.randomhouse.com/kids/

Printed in the United States of America
10 9 8 7 6 5 4 3 2

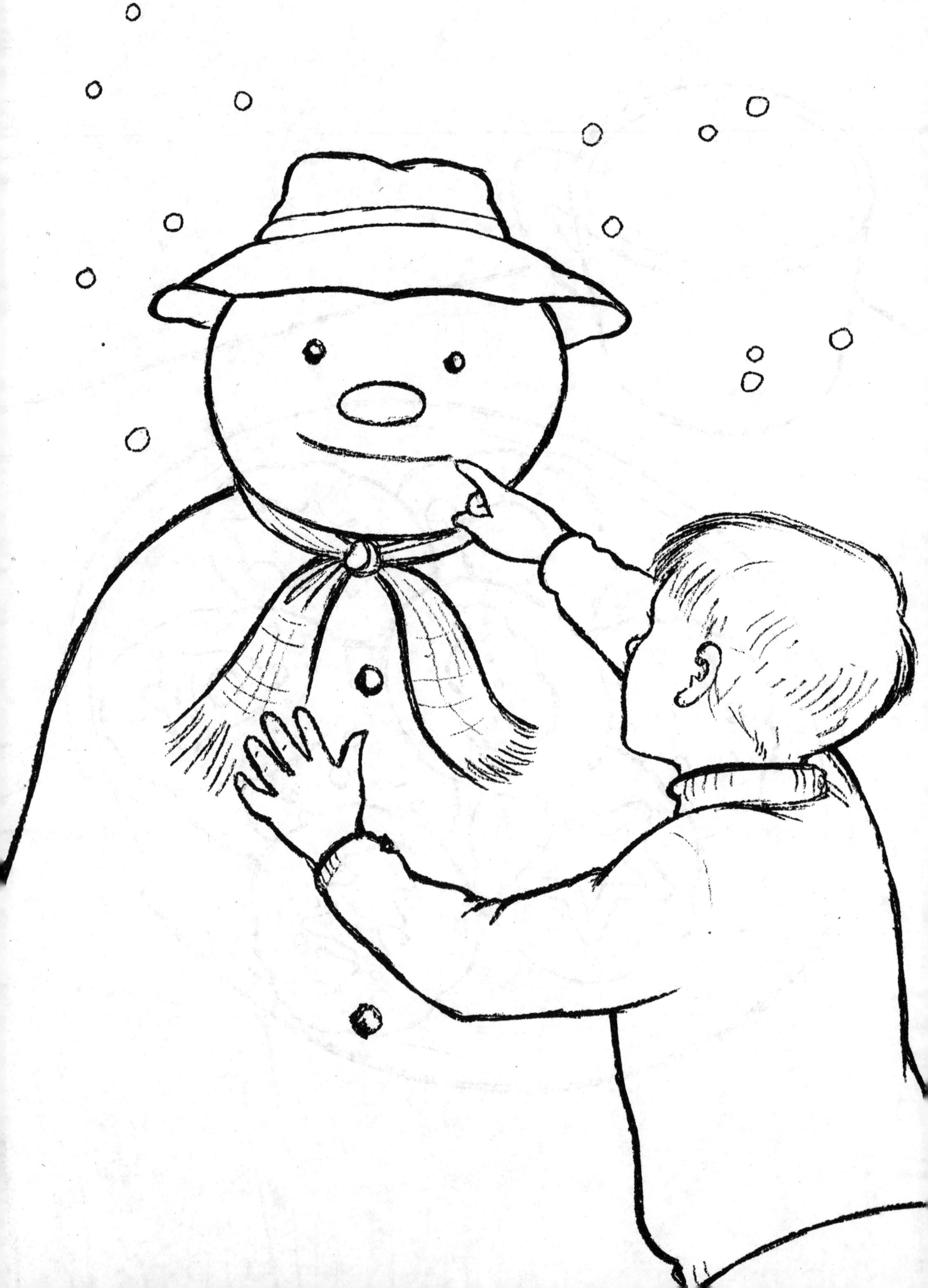

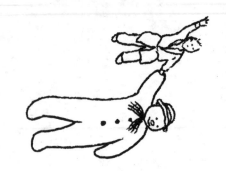

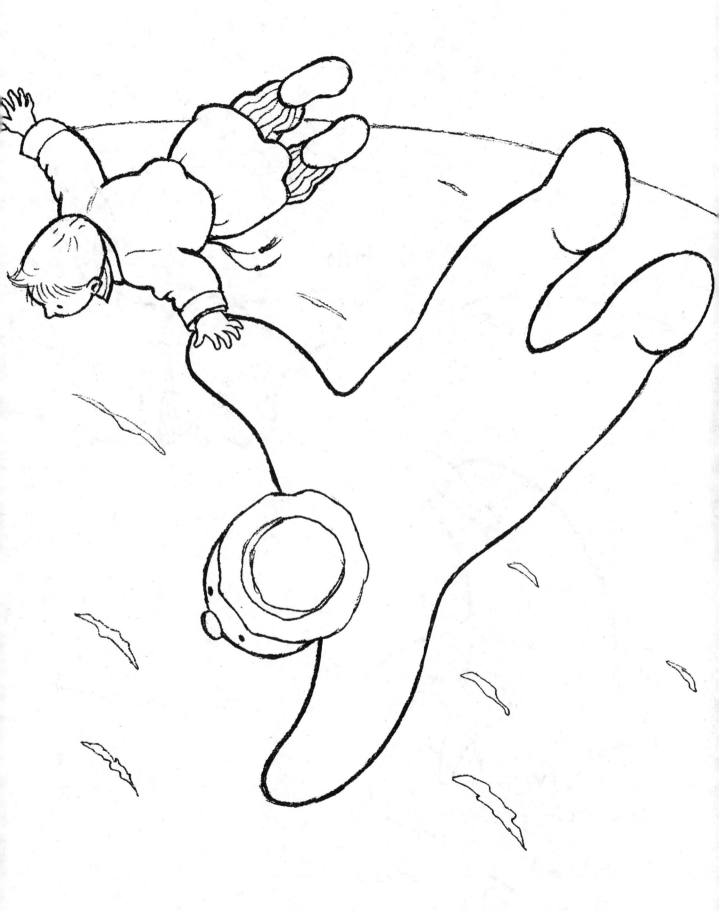

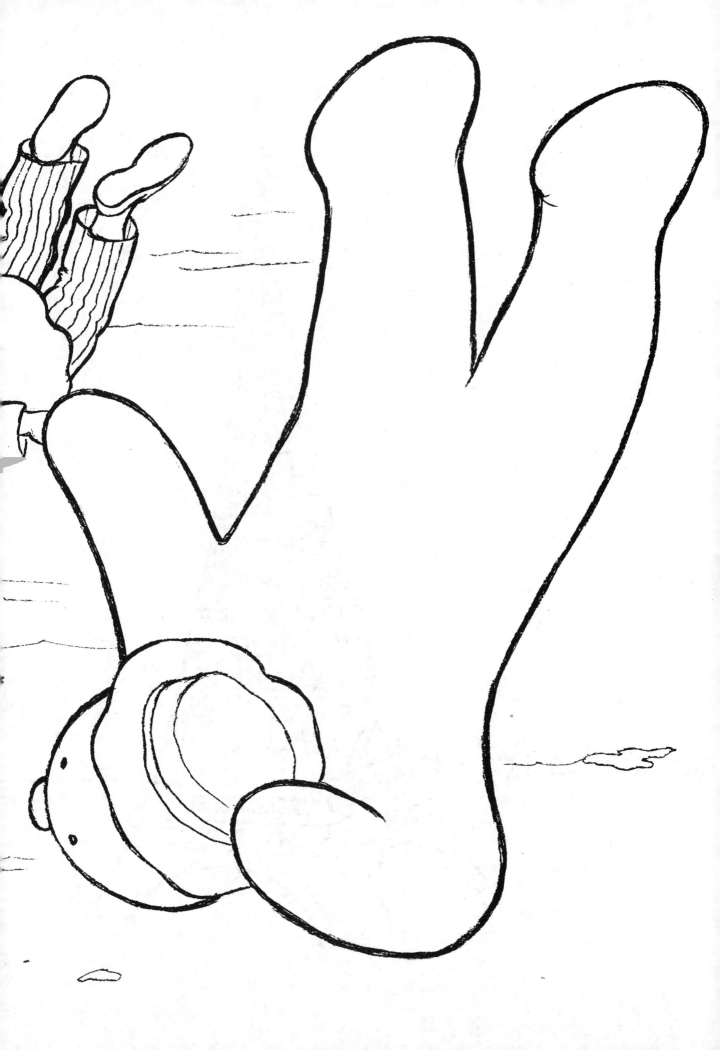

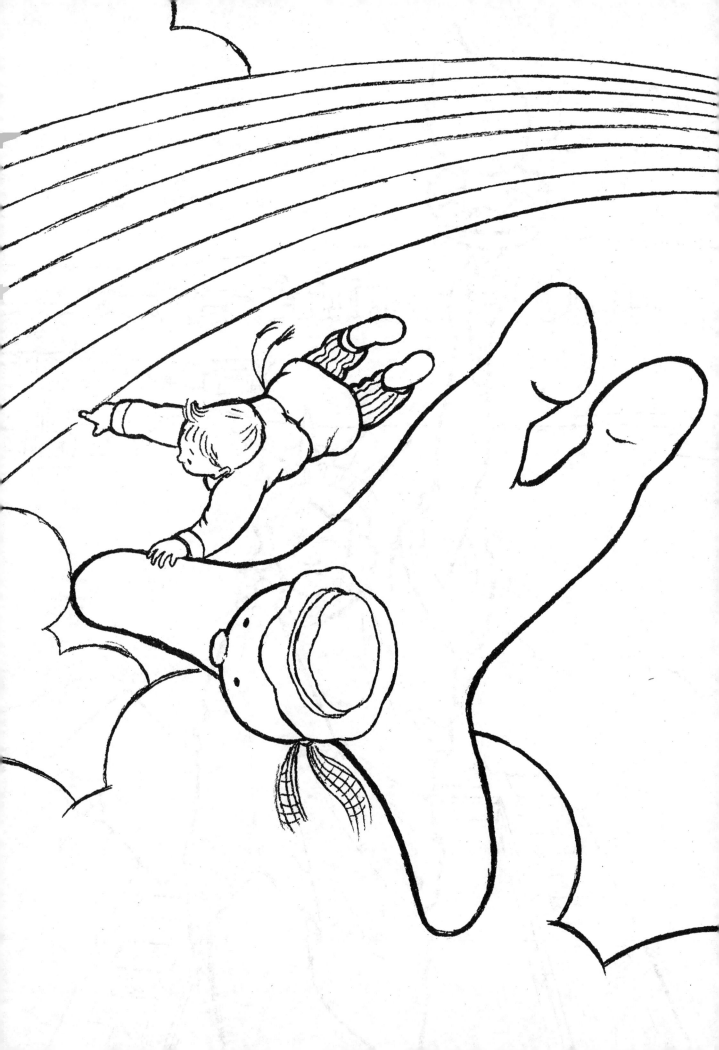

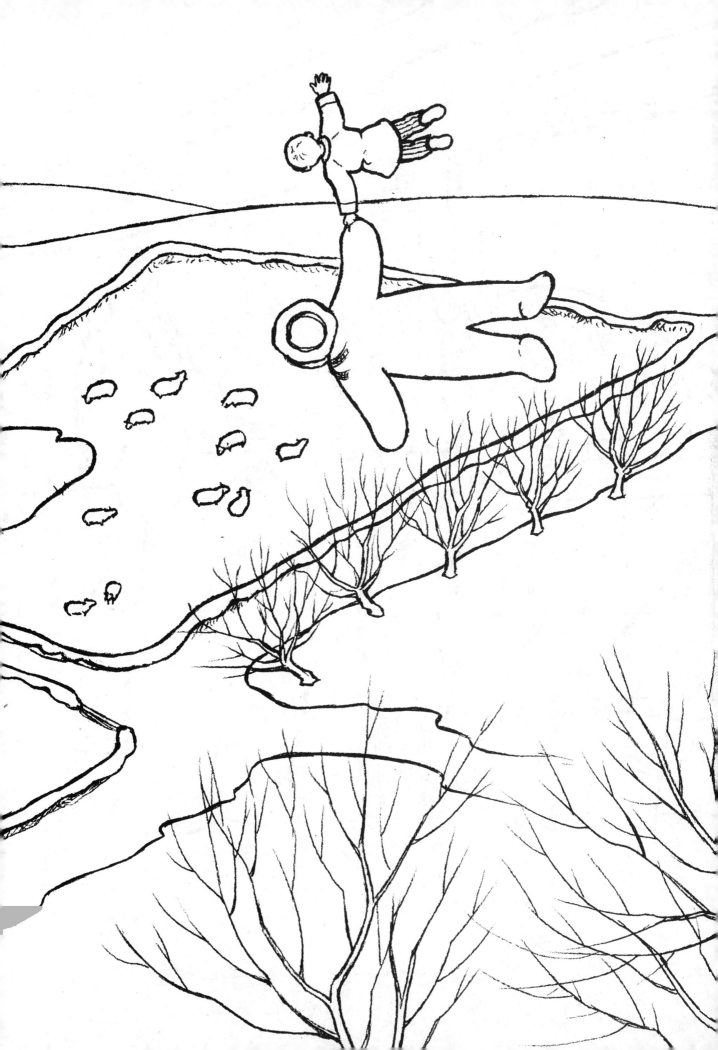